The History of Hanif Religion

(Pure Monotheistic Faith)

by

Muhammad Hamzah Sakura Ryuki

Jannah Firdaus Mediapro

2024

Jannah Firdaus Mediapro & Muhammad Hamzah Sakura Ryuki

Jannah Firdaus Mediapro & Cyber Sakura Flower Labs

Publishing
2024

Jannah Firdaus Mediapro & Muhammad Hamzah Sakura Ryuki

Prologue

Allah SWT (God) The Creator of Earth & Heaven Say:

"They say, 'Be Jews or Christians [so] you will be guided.' Say, 'Rather, [we follow] the religion of Abraham (Hanif), inclining toward truth, and he was not of the polytheists.'

Say, 'We have believed in Allah and in what was revealed to us and what was revealed to Abraham, Ishmael, Isaac, Jacob, and the Descendants, and in what was given to Moses and Jesus and to the prophets from their Lord.

We make no distinction between any of them, and we are Muslims [in submission] to Him."

(The Noble Quran Surah Al-Baqarah 2:135–136)

Hanif religion refers to the pure monotheistic beliefs practiced by certain people before the rise of Islam, particularly in the Arabian Peninsula. These individuals, known as Hanifs, rejected polytheism and idol worship, instead following the teachings of Prophet Ibrahim AS (Abraham) and believing in the existence of One God.

Although Hanifism didn't become a distinct religion, it influenced the development of Islamic theology. The Noble Quran mentions Hanifs as upright individuals who upheld pure monotheism. Today, the term "Hanif" is mainly used in historical and religious contexts, highlighting the monotheistic tradition that predates Islam and emphasizing ethical conduct and devotion to Allah SWT (God).

Jannah Firdaus Mediapro & Cyber Sakura Flower Labs

Jannah Firdaus Mediapro & Muhammad Hamzah Sakura Ryuki

Chapter 1

"Hanif" is a term that historically predates Islam and was later associated with the monotheistic beliefs of early Arab figures, particularly in the pre-Islamic Arabian Peninsula. The concept of Hanif religion has various interpretations and has evolved over time.

1. Pre-Islamic Origins:

Before the advent of Islam, the Arabian Peninsula was inhabited by various tribes practicing different forms of polytheism. Amidst this diversity, there were individuals known as Hanifs who rejected idol worship and sought a monotheistic faith. These early Hanifs are often mentioned in pre-Islamic poetry and historical accounts.

2. In Islamic Tradition:

With the emergence of Islam in the 7th century CE, the term "Hanif" gained prominence in Islamic tradition.

In Islamic sources, Hanifs are described as followers of the monotheistic faith of Prophet Ibrahim (Abraham) and are often depicted as seekers of truth who upheld moral principles even before the advent of Islam.

3. In the Quran:

The Quran, the holy book of Islam, mentions Hanifs in several verses, often in the context of praising their adherence to monotheism. For example, in Surah Al-Baqarah (2:135–136), Hanifs are described as those who have submitted themselves to God and are not among the polytheists. Similarly, in Surah Al-Hajj (22:31), Hanif is mentioned as the religion of Ibrahim, who was not a polytheist.

4. Interpretation and Legacy:

The term "Hanif" has been interpreted in various ways by scholars throughout Islamic history. Some consider it synonymous with early monotheistic beliefs, while others view it as a precursor to Islam. Hanifism, however, did not develop into a distinct religious tradition or sect; rather, it represents a moral and theological stance emphasizing monotheism and ethical conduct.

5. Modern Usage:

In contemporary discussions, the term "Hanif" may be used to refer to individuals or groups who emphasize monotheism and ethical principles in their religious or spiritual practices.

However, it remains primarily associated with its historical and Quranic context within Islam.

Overall, Hanif religion represents a historical and theological concept rooted in the monotheistic tradition of early Arab figures, particularly associated with the pre-Islamic period and the teachings of Prophet Ibrahim as depicted in Islamic scripture.

Jannah Firdaus Mediapro & Muhammad Hamzah Sakura Ryuki

Chapter 2

The ancient history of the Hanif faith traces back to the pre-Islamic era in the Arabian Peninsula.

While much of its history is shrouded in mystery and limited historical records, its significance lies in its influence on the religious and cultural landscape of the region, particularly in shaping the monotheistic tradition that eventually found expression in Islam.

To understand the ancient history of the Hanif faith, we must delve into the socio-cultural context of pre-Islamic Arabia, the figure of Prophet Ibrahim (Abraham), and the emergence of monotheistic beliefs among the early Arab tribes.

Pre-Islamic Arabia: Context and Culture

Pre-Islamic Arabia was characterized by a diverse array of tribes, each with its own religious beliefs and practices.

Polytheism was prevalent, with tribes worshipping various gods and goddesses represented by idols. Mecca, in particular, was a hub of religious activity due to the presence of the Kaaba, a sanctuary housing numerous idols revered by different tribes.

Prophet Ibrahim (Abraham) and Hanifism

The figure of Prophet Ibrahim (Abraham) holds central importance in the development of the Hanif faith.

According to Islamic tradition, Ibrahim preached monotheism in the polytheistic society of his time, challenging the prevalent idolatry and calling people to worship the one true God.

His rejection of idol worship and unwavering faith in monotheism laid the foundation for the Hanif tradition.

The Hanifs: Followers of Monotheism

Hanifs were individuals who, like Prophet Ibrahim, rejected polytheism and embraced the belief in one God. They sought spiritual purity and moral rectitude, distancing themselves from the idolatrous practices of their contemporaries.

While the term "Hanif" predates Islam and is mentioned in pre-Islamic poetry, it gained prominence with the advent of Islam as a descriptor for those who upheld monotheistic principles.

Hanifism in Pre-Islamic Poetry and Literature

Pre-Islamic poetry and literature offer glimpses into the beliefs and practices of the Hanifs. Poets such as Zuhayr ibn Abi Sulma and Labid ibn Rabi'a composed verses praising monotheism and condemning idol worship, reflecting the influence of Hanif beliefs in the cultural milieu of pre-Islamic Arabia.

Hanifism & The Noble Quran

The Noble Quran, the holy book of Islam, mentions the Hanifs in several verses, lauding their commitment to monotheism and moral integrity.

For example, Surah Al-Baqarah (2:135–136) praises the Hanifs for their devotion to God and rejection of polytheism.

Similarly, Surah Al-Hajj (22:31) refers to Hanif as the religion of Ibrahim, emphasizing his monotheistic legacy.

Influence on the Development of Islam

The Hanif tradition played a significant role in shaping the religious landscape of Arabia and laid the groundwork for the emergence of Islam. The monotheistic ideals espoused by the Hanifs found resonance in the teachings of the Prophet Muhammad, who himself traced his lineage to Prophet Ibrahim.

Islam, with its emphasis on the oneness of God and moral righteousness, drew inspiration from the Hanif tradition and incorporated elements of Hanif monotheism into its theological framework.

Legacy and Modern Interpretations

While Hanifism as an independent religious tradition faded with the rise of Islam, its legacy endures in the monotheistic principles embraced by Muslims worldwide. The term "Hanif" continues to be invoked in Islamic discourse to refer to those who uphold pure monotheism faith and strive for spiritual purity.

The ancient history of the Hanif faith serves as a testament to the enduring quest for truth and the evolution of monotheistic beliefs in the Arabian Peninsula, leaving an indelible mark on the religious and cultural heritage of the region.

Jannah Firdaus Mediapro & Muhammad Hamzah Sakura Ryuki

Chapter 3

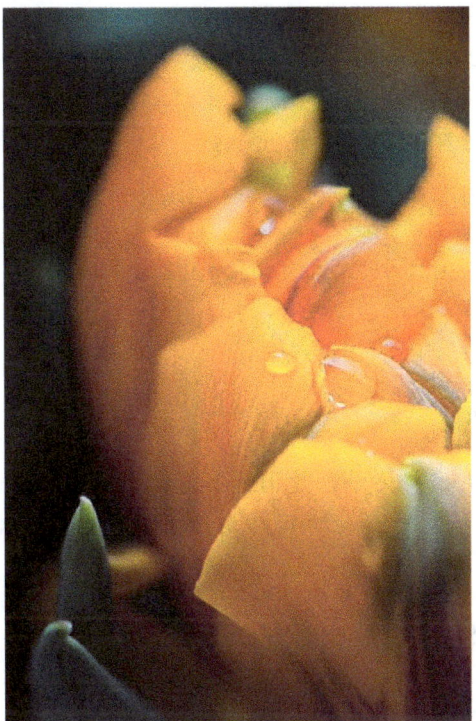

The Hanif faith, although not a structured religion in itself, embodies several core beliefs and principles based on monotheism and moral rectitude. Here are eight key points that encapsulate the essence of Hanif faith:

1. **Monotheism**:

Central to the Hanif faith is the belief in the oneness of God (Tawhid). Hanifs reject polytheism and idol worship, affirming the existence of a single, supreme deity.

2. **Primacy of Prophet Ibrahim (Abraham)**:

Hanifs revere Prophet Ibrahim as a pivotal figure who epitomized monotheism and righteousness. They uphold his legacy as a model of devotion to God and adherence to moral principles.

3. **Spiritual Purity**:

Hanif faith emphasizes spiritual purity and sincerity in worship. Followers strive for inner righteousness and integrity in their relationship with God.

4. **Rejection of Idolatry**:

Hanifs reject the worship of idols and emphasize the worship of God alone. They view idolatry as a deviation from the true path of monotheism.

5. **Ethical Conduct**:

Moral integrity is paramount in Hanif faith. Followers are encouraged to uphold principles of honesty, justice, compassion, and kindness in their interactions with others.

6. **Seeking Truth**:

Hanifs are seekers of truth who value intellectual inquiry and spiritual enlightenment. They prioritize the pursuit of knowledge and understanding in their quest for spiritual fulfillment.

7. **Submission to God**:

Hanifs believe in surrendering oneself entirely to the will of God (Islam). Submission to God's commandments and guidance is seen as the path to spiritual fulfillment and salvation.

8. **Continuity with Islam**:

While Hanifism predates Islam, it shares foundational principles with Islam, including monotheism, prophetic legacy, and moral righteousness. Hanif faith can be seen as a precursor to Islam, with many of its teachings incorporated into Islamic theology.

These eight points encapsulate the core tenets of the Hanif faith, highlighting its emphasis on monotheism, moral integrity, and devotion to God, as well as its historical significance in shaping the religious landscape of the Arabian Peninsula.

Chapter 4

While specific individuals who adhered to the Hanif faith before the advent of Islam may not be extensively documented, historical records and Islamic tradition provide insights into some notable figures who are believed to have espoused monotheistic beliefs similar to those of the Hanifs. Here are a few individuals:

1. Prophet Ibrahim (Abraham):

— **Biography**:

Ibrahim is a central figure in monotheistic traditions, revered as a prophet in Judaism, Christianity, and Islam. Born in ancient Mesopotamia, he is considered the patriarch of monotheism and is celebrated for his unwavering faith in God.

Ibrahim is credited with rejecting idol worship and preaching the worship of one true God. His willingness to sacrifice his son, as narrated in religious texts, demonstrates his profound devotion to God.

2. Zayd ibn 'Amr ibn Nufayl:

— **Biography**:

Zayd ibn 'Amr was a pre-Islamic Arab known for his rejection of idolatry and his adherence to monotheistic beliefs. He is believed to have followed the teachings of Prophet Ibrahim and advocated for the worship of one God. Zayd sought spiritual truth and righteousness, distancing himself from the idolatrous practices of his contemporaries. He is mentioned in Islamic tradition as one of the Hanifs who upheld monotheism before the advent of Islam.

3. Uthman ibn al-Huwayrith:

— **Biography**:

Uthman ibn al-Huwayrith was another figure from pre-Islamic Arabia associated with the Hanif tradition. He is said to have rejected idol worship and embraced the monotheistic faith of Prophet Ibrahim. Uthman advocated for ethical conduct and spiritual purity, embodying the principles of monotheism and righteousness. While limited historical details are available about his life, he is remembered in Islamic tradition as one of the Hanifs who preceded Islam.

4. Waraqa ibn Nawfal:

— **Biography**:

Waraqa ibn Nawfal was a cousin of Khadijah, the first wife of the Prophet Muhammad SAW. He is believed to have been a Christian scholar with knowledge of monotheistic scriptures. Waraqa is mentioned in Islamic tradition as a Hanif who rejected idol worship and anticipated the arrival of a prophet in Arabia. His monotheistic beliefs and familiarity with religious texts contributed to his recognition as a figure aligned with the Hanif tradition.

These individuals, among others, are often cited in Islamic tradition as exemplars of monotheistic faith and righteousness who lived before the advent of Islam. While their precise biographies may be shrouded in legend and historical ambiguity, their commitment to monotheism and rejection of idolatry align with the principles espoused by the Hanifs.

Author Bio

The Nameless Wandering Fragrant Wood Swordsman from The Land of Illiiyin

References

Crone, Patricia (1987). *Meccan Trade and the Rise of Islam*. Princeton University Press.

Köchler, Hans, ed. (1982). *Concept of Monotheism in Islam & Christianity*. International Progress Organization.

Monotheism. Hutchinson Encyclopedia (12th edition).

Gerhard Böwering, *God and his Attributes*, Encyclopedia of the Quran

Esposito, John L. (1998). *Islam: The Straight Path*. Oxford University Press.